AR #12099

2

W9-BRL-644

the Smallest Turtle

For a free color catalog describing Gareth Stevens' list of high-quality books and multimedia programs, call 1-800-542-2595 (USA) or 1-800-461-9120 (Canada). Gareth Stevens Publishing's Fax: (414) 225-0377.

Other GOLD STAR FIRST READER Millennium Editions:

A Dragon in a Wagon
Hairy Maclary from Donaldson's Dairy
Hairy Maclary Scattercat
Hairy Maclary and Zachary Quack
Hairy Maclary's Caterwaul Caper
Hairy Maclary's Rumpus at the Vet
SNIFF-SNUFF-SNAP!

and also by Lynley Dodd:

Hairy Maclary, Sit
Hairy Maclary's Showbusiness
The Minister's Cat ABC
Schnitzel von Krumm Forget-Me-Not
Slinky Malinki Catflaps

Library of Congress Cataloging-in-Publication Data

Dodd, Lynley.
    The smallest turtle / by Lynley Dodd.
        p. cm. — (Gold star first readers)
    Summary: A newly-hatched turtle makes the dangerous journey across a beach full of obstacles to the nearby sea.
    ISBN 0-8368-2692-2 (lib. bdg.)
    1. Turtles—Juvenile fiction. [1. Turtles—Fiction. 2. Seashore—Fiction.] I. Title. II. Series.
PZ10.3.D71048Sm   2000
[E]—dc21   00-029174

This edition first published in 2000 by
Gareth Stevens Publishing
A World Almanac Education Group Company
1555 North RiverCenter Drive, Suite 201
Milwaukee, WI 53212 USA

First published in New Zealand by Mallinson Rendel Publishers Ltd. Original © 1982 by Lynley Dodd.

Printed in the United States of America

1 2 3 4 5 6 7 8 9 04 03 02 01 00

the Smallest Turtle

Lyrley·Dodd

Gareth Stevens Publishing
A WORLD ALMANAC EDUCATION GROUP COMPANY

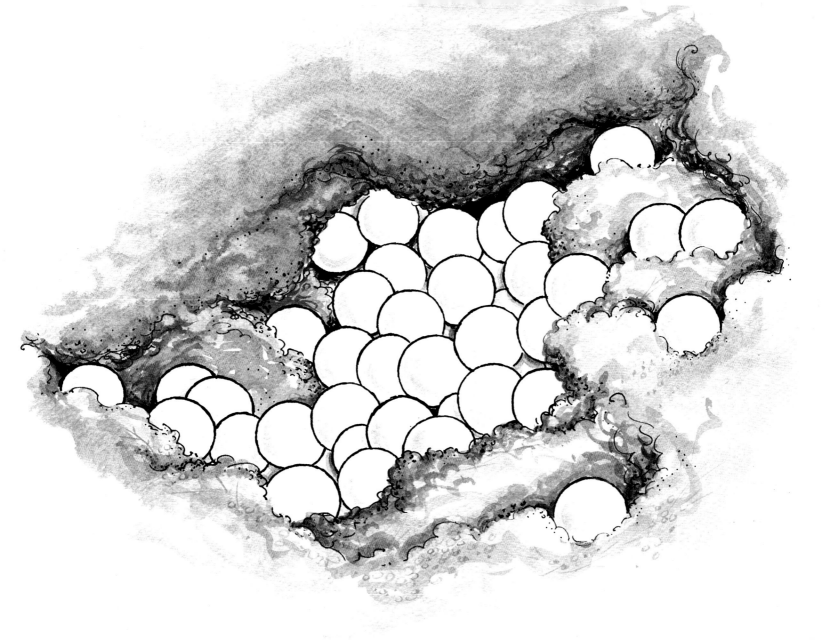

Deep in a safe, dark hole
under the sand
lay a nest of turtle eggs.

One day,
they began to hatch.
Soon there were
dozens of baby turtles
all wriggling together
up through the sand
and away.

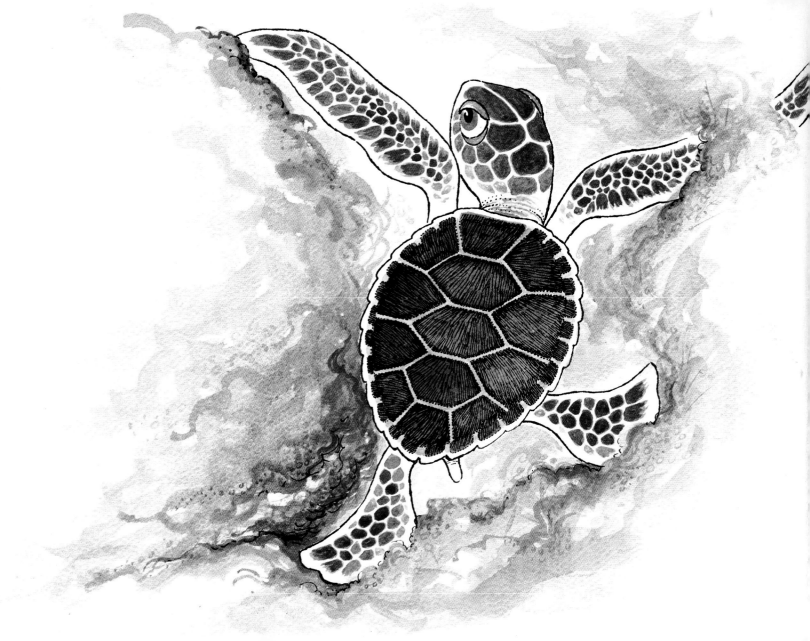

Except the smallest turtle.
He was late.
All by himself
he scrambled and scrabbled
up, up, up . . .

and out into the shimmery sun.
He blinked at the brightness
and inside his head he heard strange words,
"To the sea — to the sea."

So away he went,
skitterscatter,
over a shiny, gray rock
and past a big, black beetle,

around a tree with twisty roots,

down a gravelly hole
and up the other side,
where a sleepy lizard
was dozing in the sun,

through some prickly grass
where a spider was weaving a web
and all the time, his head said,
"To the sea — to the sea."

The sun was burning down
on the smallest turtle.
It made him too hot
and it muddled the words in his head.
He began to go round and round
in circles.

He crept into the shade
of a big, green leaf
to cool down
and as he cooled,
the words in his head
slowly came back again,
"To the sea — to the sea."

So on and on went the smallest turtle
until at last he stopped to rest.
He was getting very tired.
Suddenly he heard something.
It was the sound of waves
crashing and hissing on the sand.
The words in his head became stronger than ever,
"To the SEA — to the SEA."

But there was danger.
Gulls were wheeling and whirling
up in the sky,
looking with beady, greedy eyes
for a baby turtle lunch.

The smallest turtle didn't wait.
Down the scorching sand he scrabbled and skittered,
faster, faster,
away from the gulls,
past the crabs,
over the seaweed,
over the shells,
over the stones and . . .

at last he felt cool, cool water
on his hot, tired, sandy body.
And as he swam down,
down,
down,
he knew.
"It's the SEA," he sang,
"It's the SEA!"

Acknowledgement
This book was written with the assistance of the Choysa Bursary,
funded jointly by Quality Packers Ltd. and the New Zealand Literary Fund.
The author gratefully acknowledges their support.